# THIS BOOK BELONGS TO:

_____

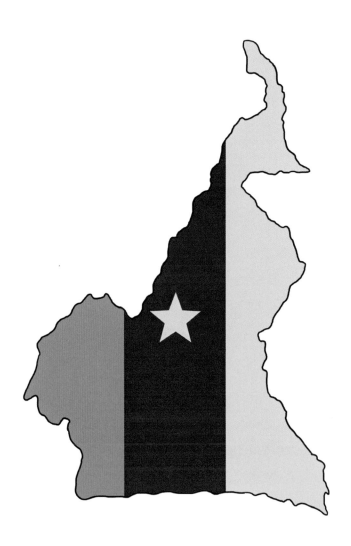

Cameroon, The Majestic Little Africa

# The Prince
## and the
# The Lioness

ISBN: 979-8-378546-70-1 (Paperback) | ISBN: 978-1-949757-16-3 (Hardcover)

First Printing 2023

NDE MEDIA GROUP
NOBILITY, DIGNITY, ELEGANCE

www.snowflowerbooks.com

*For my children - Jules, Louis and Marguerite.*

And for the world. I pray for all living beings to be free, for all living beings to be happy, for all living beings to find their existential purpose, and for all living beings to realize their sublime nature.

"In the beginning was the Word,
and the Word was with God,
and the Word was God.

– John 1:1

It was a hot day in the Cameroonian village where Snow Flower lived with her grandma, Mamie Marguerite. Snow Flower was sitting on the verandah with Nzui stretched out beside her. *What a beautiful black panther he is*, she thought. He had grown so much since she'd rescued him from a hunter's trap in the forest.

A gentle breeze rustled the dry leaves of the trees, and a lizard stood on the step soaking up the sun. Snow could hear Mamie singing in the kitchen as she flipped sliced plantains in the frying pan. Snow felt happy from head to toe.

She was wondering how they might spend the afternoon when she remembered the book she had borrowed. Mrs. Kamga had asked her class to read a story and draw a picture, which would be displayed on the classroom wall.

Snow had chosen *The Prince and the Lioness* from the school library. The book was in her backpack in her bedroom.

She returned with it tucked tightly under one arm as she tried not to spill her glass of mango juice and a dish of water for Nzui.

"Can I read this story to you, Nzui?" she asked. "I think you will enjoy it."

"Yes, please do, Snow." He lapped up his water with his long pink tongue, then settled down to listen.

Snow opened the book and read aloud.

Once upon a time, there was a chief who led a small village near the African bush. The chief had many sons.

His oldest son, Prince Jelani, was the best hunter in all the land, and whenever he went out hunting, he always came back with more meat than any hunter in the village. It was often more meat than all the villagers could eat.

In truth, Prince Jelani didn't just hunt animals for food; he took great pleasure in stalking his prey and outsmarting it— the prince hunted animals for fun.

The chief was angry with his son, and ashamed too.
The chief knew that the spirits of the land did not approve of his son's unnecessary cruelty towards the animals of the African bush, but the chief's wise words fell on deaf ears.
His son the prince would not change his ways.

The animals were also angry with the prince. They were afraid of him, too. They wanted to stop him, so they called a meeting in the bush. Animals big and small came from far and wide: elephants, giraffes, zebras, lions, cheetahs, baboons, chimpanzees, meerkats, squirrels— they all wanted to work together to try and stop the prince.

"We could set a trap to catch him," said the elephant with the longest tusks. But the animals agreed that this prince was too clever to fall into a trap.

"He would spot it from afar," said the tallest meerkat, standing on her hind legs to see better.

"One of us could change into a beautiful woman," said the largest lion with the bushiest mane. He was the king of the lions. "The prince could be lured into the forest if the woman pretended to be lost. Then, we could punish him for his cruelty."

"Yes!" said the animals, excited by the king lion's plan.

They decided that the king lion's daughter, the lioness named Princess Asha, would trick the prince. But Princess Asha wasn't so sure about this plan. She wanted the prince to stop hunting so many animals, but hurting him would make the animals just as cruel as the hunter. She wanted to say this, but the lion princess wasn't brave enough to speak out.

The next morning, the chief's son was getting ready for his daily hunt. He was gathering his weapons – a spear and bow and arrows – when his father tried to stop him.

"Son, stay home today," said the chief. "I had a dream that you went into the bush and you didn't come back."

His son scoffed. "Dreams are just thoughts, father, nothing more."

"But in my dream, you were attacked by a lion! Stay home today," begged the chief.

"Pah! Don't be ridiculous. I can take care of myself," said Jelani, raising his spear. "I can stop any beast that tries to hurt me." He pushed his pleading father aside and set off.

The prince had a good day in the bush. When he had hunted as much meat as he could carry, he decided to call it a day.

He was making his way back home when, to his surprise, he saw a young woman coming towards him.

"Sister, what are you doing in the bush? I can see you are not from our village."

She smiled. "My name is Princess Asha. I have heard stories of a prince who is one of the greatest hunters in all the land," she said. "So, I decided to find you and see for myself."

"I am on my way home," said the prince. "Why don't you come with me. After we have had something to eat and drink, I can take you safely back to your village."

The chief welcomed the princess to his village. They ate a hearty meal and enjoyed each other's company.

Afterwards, the prince was gathering his weapons for the journey back to the princess's village when she stopped him. "If you take your weapons, my father will think you have come to fight," she said.

Prince Jelani agreed it would be wrong to turn up with his spear, so they set off through the bush unarmed. When they were still some distance from the village, the woman said she would go on ahead to let her father know the prince was coming.

When she was out of sight, the young woman changed back into the lioness and hid behind a tree like her father had told her to, waiting to pounce on the unsuspecting prince. But when he arrived, she just couldn't bring herself to hurt him. So, she decided that she would scare him instead.

She creeped out of the brush, snarling and crawling towards him. The prince gasped! He thought he was done for. Then, the lioness pounced, knocking Prince Jelani to the ground with her strong paws. He looked deep into the eyes of the lioness, which he thought looked strangely familiar...

The lioness gave a mighty roar so that all the jungle could hear. With her forceful, angry growl, she tried to tell the prince to stop hunting her animals so cruelly, but she couldn't speak the language of humans in her lioness form.

Just as suddenly as she had appeared, she left him. Though he was unharmed, he was completely stunned. Prince Jelani sat still in shock. He was mystified by this strange encounter with such a beautiful and mighty animal. He should not have been alive, and he didn't know how to feel about it.

A short while later, the lioness returned in the form of Princess Asha to find the prince sitting silently.

He looked shaken and sad. He declared the bush was too dangerous and said they would have to return to her village another day.

It was almost dark when they returned to his village. The chief had grown sick with worry.

"Father," said Prince Jelani, "We were attacked by a lioness. But she didn't hurt me like you said she would. I don't know what to do. A part of me feels I should hunt her for revenge, but somehow that doesn't seem right. The lioness was so beautiful, and it was almost like she wanted to tell me something..."

Princess Asha realized that this was her final chance to use her voice. She would have to be brave and speak her mind for the sake of the animals of the African bush.

"Prince Jelani, my people revere and respect the animals of the jungle. That lion was only trying to defend its land and kin. If we do not respect the animals, they will only act out of anger and fear towards us humans."

Prince Jelani had to think on these words. Never before had he thought of the matter in this way, and never before had he heard someone defend the animals as if they were equals to humans. He did not say that he agreed, but he went to bed with new, strange thoughts in his mind.

He woke up the next day and, for the first time in years, he had no desire to hunt. He saw all the meat he had gathered for the villagers and realized it was plenty to keep them healthy and happy for a long time to come. He thought that, instead, he would spend the day with his people and help them with other important matters, like fixing their rooftops and teaching the village children their ancestral ways.

The next day, Prince Jelani declared to Princess Asha and his father, "I will not hunt again until we have need for more meat for our people. Princess Asha, thank you for explaining the importance of living in harmony with the animals of our kingdom. Would you do me the honor of introducing me to your people? I would like to learn your ways."

"I am so happy to hear you have had a change of heart," said Princess Asha. She and Prince Jelani set off to meet her father. This time, the prince did not even think about taking his weapons, and the princess did not change back into a lioness. They set off through the jungle until they came upon a clearing. The prince stopped short.

"Princess Asha, this is not safe. Look, there are lions!" said Prince Jelani.

"Yes, I know," said Princess Asha with a smile. "These lions are my people."

When the prince met the pride of lions, he saw up close how magnificent they were. And when he found out that the young woman was the princess of the animal kingdom, and daughter of the king lion, his heart filled with kindness for all the animals.

He looked to Princess Asha in amazement and his heart filled with love. "I recognize you now. You were the lioness who I met in the forest. You could have killed me, but you didn't. I can tell who you are by your beautiful lioness eyes."

The prince and the lioness smiled at one another; they knew it was the start of a harmonious relationship between humans and the animal kingdom.

The two eventually fell in love and were married, uniting humans with the animals. Prince Jelani vowed to live differently. He would live peacefully with the animals that shared the bush with the villagers. From that day forward, he would show kindness and love, and he would care about the land and all its inhabitants, especially his new lion princess and her animal kingdom.

"That's the end of the story, Nzui!" said Snow. "I love that Prince Jelani learns the importance of respecting the land and its animals, and I really love that Princess Asha learns to use her voice to stand up for what she believes in. What do you think, Nzui?"

She closed the book and looked down to find that the panther was gently sleeping. She hoped Nzui hadn't missed the ending. Maybe she would wake him up and read the story all over again!

**DID YOU KNOW....?**

A lion can run short distances at

**50 mph**

and <u>leap</u> as far as

**36 feet!**

**DID YOU KNOW....?**

Male lions **defend** the pride's territory while lionesses do the **hunting.**

DID YOU KNOW....?

Lions are the most social of all big cats and live together in **prides.**

A pride consists of about **fifteen** lions, lionesses, and their little cubs.

## Books Mission Statement

Snow Flower Books was founded by Fleurie Leclercq, who grew up in the village of Yaounde in Cameroon, Africa. She wrote her first book, *Snow Flower and the Panther*, in order to showcase her African culture through the eyes of a young girl living day by day with pride in her heritage and community. Fleurie's stories explore what it means to grow up with a true village mentality: understanding the value of togetherness, kindness, and sharing your purpose with those around you.

Snow Flower Books envisions a future full of self-expression, unconditional love, and balance between people and the planet. Join us on our mission to empower children of all backgrounds to discover their inner-light and share it with the world in order to make it a more kind and beautiful place. And remember: it takes a village; so spread the love.

# OTHER BOOKS BY FLEURIE LECLERCQ

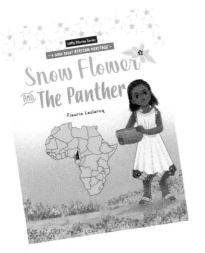

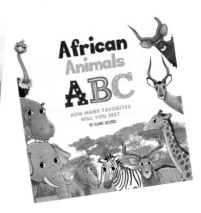

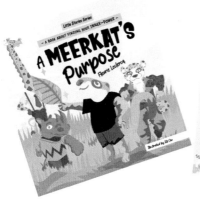

## Also available in SPANISH and FRENCH!

Check out our best selling series at

www.snowflowerbooks.com

Available on Amazon.com

 @snowflowervillage   Snow Flower Books

 @fleurie_author   Fleurie Leclercq

Made in the USA
Middletown, DE
01 March 2023

25869327R00031